FAIRY TALE LUNCHES
A COOKBOOK FOR
YOUNG READERS AND EATERS

Fairy Tales retold by

Jane Yolen

Recipes by

Heidi E.Y. Stemple

Illustrations by

Philippe Béha

an imprint of
WINDMILL BOOKS
New York

For my daughter, for meals cooked, jokes shared, and love always
—JY

For Jen and the thousands of dinners we cooked together, for Nina whose name should
be on this book for all the help she gave me, and for all my taste testers especially my
daughters—Maddison and Glendon
—HEYS

For my daughters Sara and Fanny
—PB

The recipes in this book are intended to be prepared with an adult's help.

Published in 2010 by Windmill Books, LLC

303 Park Avenue South, Suite # 1280, New York, NY 10010-3657

Adaptations to school & library edition © 2010 Windmill Books

Adapted from *Fairy Tale Feasts: A Literary Cookbook for Young Readers and Eaters.*

Published by arrangement with Crocodile Books, an imprint of Interlink Publishing Group, Inc.

Text copyright © 2006 Jane Yolen and Heidi E. Y. Stemple

Illustrations copyright © 2006 Philippe Béha

Publisher Cataloging Data

Yolen, Jane

        Fairy tale lunches : a cookbook for young readers and eaters. – School & library ed. / fairy tales retold by Jane Yolen ; recipes by Heidi E. Y. Stemple ; illustrations by Philippe Béha.

        p. cm. – (Fairy tale cookbooks)

        Contents: Little Red Riding Hood–The magic cave–The fox and the grapes–The stolen bread smells.

        Summary: This book includes retellings of four fairy tales paired with lunch recipes connected to each story.

        ISBN 978-1-60754-576-7 (lib.) – ISBN 978-1-60754-577-4 (pbk.)

ISBN 978-1-60754-579-8 (6-pack)

        1. Cookery–Juvenile literature   2. Luncheons–Juvenile literature   3. Fairy tales   [1. Cookery   2. Luncheons   3. Fairy tales]   I. Stemple, Heidi E. Y.   II. Béha, Philippe   III. Title   IV. Series

        641.5/123–dc22

Manufactured in the United States of America.

TABLE OF CONTENTS

STORIES AND STOVETOPS:
AN INTRODUCTION

From the earliest days of stories, when hunters came home from the hunt to tell of their exploits around the campfire while gnawing on a leg of beast, to the era of kings in castles listening to the storyteller at the royal dinner feast, to the time of TV dinners when whole families gathered to eat and watch movies together, stories and eating have been close companions.

So it is not unusual that folk stories are often about food: Jack's milk cow traded for beans, Snow White given a poisoned apple, a pancake running away from those who would eat it.

But there is something more—and this is about the powerful ties between stories and recipes. Both are changeable, suiting the need of the maker and the consumer.

A storyteller never tells the same story twice, because every audience needs a slightly different story, depending upon the season or the time of day, the restlessness of the youngest listener, or how appropriate a tale is to what has just happened in the storyteller's world. And every cook knows that a recipe changes according to the time of day, the weather, the altitude, the number of grains in the level teaspoonful, the ingredients found (or not found) in the cupboard or refrigerator, the tastes or allergies of the dinner guests, even the cook's own feelings about the look of the batter.

So if you want to tell these stories yourself or make these recipes yourself, be playful. After first making them exactly as they are in this book, you can begin to experiment. Recipes, like stories, are made more beautiful by what *you* add to them. Add, subtract, change, try new ways. We have, and we expect you will, too. In fact, in the recipes, we have already given you some alternatives, like different toppings and other spices.

–Jane Yolen and Heidi E.Y. Stemple

LITTLE RED RIDING HOOD

Once upon a time there was a little girl who was loved by everyone who knew her, but the one who loved her best was her grandmother. In fact, her Granny made the little girl a riding hood of red velvet, and after that the child was never seen without it.

Now one day Red Riding Hood's mother said, "I have packed some sandwiches and other goodies in a picnic basket for you to take to Granny. She has been sick and they will do her good. Now, mind you, don't dawdle in the woods."

"I'll go right along," Red Riding Hood answered, and she meant it at the time. But once she got into the woods, it was such a lovely day she decided to pick some flowers to go with the basket of goodies. While she was dawdling, along came a handsome wolf.

Not knowing what a wicked creature he was, Red Riding Hood had no more fear of him than if he had been a large dog. And as this was once upon a time, the wolf could talk.

"Where are you going, Little Red Riding Hood?" asked he.

"To my Granny's" she answered.

There are three basic versions of the Little Red Riding Hood story. In one, the wolf eats her and the story is over. In a second, the woodsman or hunter shows up in time and rescues Red (and sometimes Granny as well.) In the third, both Red and Granny are eaten, but the woodsman finds the wolf and knocks him out. When he cuts the wolf open, he discovers both Red and Granny alive. Out they come and place large stones in the wolf's belly, then sew him up again. When the wolf wakes up, he is very thirsty and goes off to a river, but the stones in his belly are so heavy, he falls in the river and drowns.

"And what's in your picnic basket?" he asked.

"Sandwiches and other goodies," she said. "To give her strength."

"I'm sure it will," said the wolf. "And where does Granny live?"

Suspecting nothing, she told him. He bid her good day and showed her where some exceedingly beautiful trillium grew, down by the brook, then off he went. So Little Red Riding Hood picked flowers until she had a great bouquet of them. Then she got back on the path and headed toward Granny's.

But the wolf had been there before her. He had knocked on the door and when Granny asked, "Who is there?" he had imitated her granddaughter's voice. "Little Red Riding Hood."

"Lift the latch," Granny called out in a tiny voice, "for I am too weak to rise."

The wolf lifted the latch, went inside, leaped onto the bed, and swallowed the old lady whole. Then he put on her extra cap and gown and lay down on the bed, drawing up the quilt to cover himself completely.

Not five minutes later, in came Little Red Riding Hood. "Good morning, Granny," she called. "I have a bunch of flowers and a picnic basket quite full of sandwiches and other goodies."

"Set them on the floor," said the wolf, trying to disguise his voice.

"Grandmother, what a rough voice you have," said Little Red Riding Hood.

"That's my cold speaking," whispered the wolf.

The girl came toward the bed and saw the hairy creature in her grandmother's cap. "Why, grandmother, what big ears you have."

"The better to hear you with, my dear."

She came closer. "Why, grandmother, what big eyes you have."

"The better to see you with my dear."

She stood at the side of the bed. "Why, grandmother, what big teeth you have."

"The better to eat you with, my dear!" And saying this, the wolf threw aside the covers and leaped out of bed.

Screaming, Little Red Riding Hood ran toward the door and that very moment, the door was flung open. In stepped a hunter who that very morning had been tracking the wolf.

"Why, you old sinner, I have you now," he cried, aiming his gun and shooting the wolf dead. And when he went to fillet the wolf, who should he find but Granny, still very much alive, though his knife had cut away her white curls.

So Red Riding Hood learned not to stray off the path, the grandmother learned to keep her door bolted, and the hunter— well, he learned to fillet wolves very, very carefully. ⭐

The most familiar version of this story comes from the Brothers Grimm where it is called "Little Red Cap." However, the earliest published version is in Perrault's 1697 Histories or Tales of Times Past.

The famous writer Charles Dickens wrote that Red Riding Hood had been his first love. "I felt that if I could have married Little Red Riding Hood, I should have known perfect bliss." He would have read the English version that first appeared in 1729.

Little Red Riding Hood's Picnic Basket of Goodies

Good enough for Granny or a party of hungry wolves.

Deviled Eggs
(Makes 12 yummy eggs)

EQUIPMENT:
- pan
- slotted spoon or colander
- bowl and spoon or food processor
- spoon or icing bag with a large star tip

INGREDIENTS:
- 6 eggs
- ¼ cup mayonnaise (60 ml)
- ½ tsp. dried mustard
- salt and pepper to taste
- paprika

DIRECTIONS:

1. Place the eggs carefully in the pan, cover with cold water and bring to a boil over high heat. Lower the heat to medium-high and boil for 12 minutes.

2. Remove from water with a slotted spoon or by pouring gently into a colander, and let cool.

3. Peel eggs and cut each one in half lengthwise.

4. Gently scoop out the yolks and put them, the mayonnaise, salt, pepper, and dried mustard in the bowl or food processor. Blend until creamy. Add more mayonnaise if necessary. Hint: Always start with less mayonnaise than you need because you can always add more, but you cannot take any out.

5. Scoop the yolk mixture back into the eggs with a spoon or pipe it in through the pastry bag.

6. Top with a small sprinkle of paprika.

VARIATIONS:

Try topping with a slice of green olive or a sprig of fresh parsley instead of paprika. 🍅

Act of 1871—was passed because it gave working people time off from their jobs.
4. A picnic basket is also called a picnic hamper.
5. Picnic baskets can come equipped with fine china, silverware, and linen napkins. You have to make the food yourself.
6. Now picnics are big business, and along with the many varieties of picnic baskets, you can also buy picnic tables, picnic backpacks, and insulated coolers. Or you can just carry everything in a paper bag and bring along your fingers and a hearty appetite.

Chicken Salad Pockets

The better to eat, my dear. (Makes 6–7 servings)

For this recipe you can use leftover chicken instead of preparing an entire chicken. Just remember: if you are using a smaller amount of leftover chicken, lessen the amounts of the other ingredients too.

EQUIPMENT:

- large stockpot

- large serving fork or tongs

- large bowl

- knife

- cutting board

- peeler

- large spoon

- measuring cup

INGREDIENTS:

- 1 whole chicken

- ½ cup mayonnaise (120 ml)

- 1 large celery stalk, chopped

- 1 green apple, cubed and tossed with a sprinkle of lemon juice

- 1 tsp. lemon juice plus more for sprinkling on the apple

- 1 tsp. balsamic vinegar

- ¼ cup chopped walnuts (40 g)

- salt and pepper to taste

- pita bread

- Brie cheese (optional)

DIRECTIONS:

1. Remove the giblets (liver and other parts in a plastic bag) from inside the chicken and throw out (or set aside if someone will use them later). Rinse the chicken in cool water and place it in a large stock pot. Fill with water to cover the chicken, sprinkle in some salt and pepper, and bring to a boil over high heat. Lower to medium heat and cook for an hour. Remove chicken carefully with a large serving fork, tongs, or both, and set aside to cool. When cool, remove all the meat from the bones with your fingers and a knife. Chop the meat into small pieces. This makes about 4 cups and can be replaced with leftover chicken. The chicken stock left in the pot can be saved for another recipe or frozen.

2. Mix chicken and mayonnaise in large bowl.

3. Wash and chop celery and peel, chop, and toss the apple with lemon juice so it does not turn brown.

4. Add the apple, celery, salt, pepper, lemon juice, vinegar, and walnuts to the chicken mixture and toss together.

5. Cut the top inch from each piece of pita bread.

6. Spread the Brie on the inside of each pocket with a butter knife.

7. Fill with chicken salad and serve.

THE MAGIC CAVE

Once near a small Polish village there lived a poor Jewish farmer named Shimon and his wife, Gert. Though they had no money, they never cursed their fate. Rather they would go to the synagogue every Sabbath and pray.

"For though we have little," Shimon said to his wife, "we have more than many."

And indeed they did. They had two goats that gave them milk—a little but enough—and with the goat's milk they made butter and cheese for themselves and some to sell at market.

A little—but enough.

Now one evening, when Gert went to bring in the goats from the field, they were not there. Gone. Vanished.

Shimon and Gert searched high, they searched low, they searched all the fields around, but the goats were nowhere to be found.

Then Gert began to weep into her apron but Shimon said, "Everything is from Heaven. We do not yet know what this means."

"Means?" cried Gert, "it means we will go hungry." But she stopped her wailing long enough to go into the house and to light the evening's candles.

Just then Shimon ran in shouting, "They have come home. And see! See!"

Gert ran outside and sure enough, there were the goats, their udders swollen with milk. And when Gert milked them, there was twice as much milk as ever before. "Oh my husband, how right you are. Everything indeed, is from Heaven!"

• • •

Well, the next evening it was the same. The goats vanished from the fields and could not be found. But after the candles were lit, they suddenly appeared at the barn door, their udders swollen with milk, more milk than ever.

"A miracle!" said Shimon, and Gert agreed.

And even more miraculous, the milk seemed to heal the sick, and the cheese to cure the dying. Soon no one in the little village had so much as a hangnail.

• • •

Six days passed, miracle after miracle. But on the seventh day, Shimon said to Gert, "I must follow the goats and see where they go. For what if this miracle is of the devil's making?"

"Good healing milk could never be from the Evil One," said Gert, spitting through her fingers to ward off the wicked one.

16

"But husband, if you are determined to go, I will go with you. Nothing should separate a man and his wife."

So they followed the goats around the field and through a forest that was wide in some places and narrow in others. They climbed after them when the goats went up the mountain. And at last, they followed the goats into a dark cave.

"Hold onto my coattails," Shimon said as they entered the cave. "Do not be afraid." He did not say that he was a little afraid himself. "Heaven will protect us."

They had gone but a little way into the cave when they saw afar a bright, shining light. The goats scrambled ahead toward the light and Shimon and Gert followed after.

Suddenly devils and imps leaped out at them. Stones rained down from the cave walls.

"Do not be afraid," whispered Gert in Shimon's ear. "Heaven will protect us."

A number of the parts of this story can be found as traveling motifs in other stories, including: Underground Passage Magically Opens, Journey to an Earthly Paradise, and Treasure-Producing Goat.

This reminder heartened Shimon and so the two went ahead, looking neither left nor right. When the devils and imps saw they could make no impression on the two—nor separate them—they disappeared back to the dark regions of dreams.

Shimon and Gert followed the goats all the way to the light, and then through it. When they came out the other side of the cave, they found themselves standing in a green and fertile valley.

Nearby was a young shepherd, playing on his pipe.

"Who are you?" asked Shimon.

"And where are we?" asked Gert.

The shepherd boy took the pipe from his mouth. "My name is Dov," he said. "And down there," he thrust out his hand, "is the holy city of Jerusalem."

How strange! From Poland to Jerusalem is a long and arduous trip. It takes many months of walking. Yet here they were!

"A miracle indeed," said Shimon to Gert. "Let us tell all our cousins to follow the goats here to the Holy Land."

So they wrote a letter to the people of the town, wrapped the letter in a fig leaf, and tied the fig leaf to one of the goats.

That night the goats went back through the cave to Poland. They were found the next day by a man who lived in the village, but he did not notice the fig leaf. Instead he knocked on the door of the house but old Shimon and Gert were gone.

For six days the villager came to check on them, but they never came back. Fearing the worst, he took the goats to his house, but as they could not be cared for in town, they were taken to the slaughterhouse where they were killed for their meat. Only then was the note found—too late. The goats could no longer show the people of the town how to find the cave.

So the rabbi kept the letter in the synagogue, and when he died, it was in the keeping of the next rabbi. And finally, when the little town was burned down in the Great Holocaust, the letter was gone as well.

And all that is left is this story. ⭐

Goat Cheese Sandwiches

So delicious, you'll think you're in heaven. (Serves 2–3)

EQUIPMENT:

• cutting board

• sharp knife

• peeler (optional)

• clean scissors (optional)

• measuring spoons

• small bowl

• whisk or fork

• spoon

• butter knife

INGREDIENTS:

• 1 12-inch (30 cm) baguette or other unsliced bread

• 3 small tomatoes or 1 large tomato

• 1 cucumber (medium-sized or half a larger one)

• 6 fresh basil leaves

• 1 tbsp. balsamic vinegar

• 1 tbsp. extra virgin olive oil

• dash of salt

• dash of pepper

• 4 oz. mild goat cheese (120 g)

• slices of purple onion (optional)

DIRECTIONS:

1. Slice the tomatoes. Peel and slice the cucumber. Cut the basil leaves into strips with scissors or a knife and set them all aside.

2. Cut the bread lengthwise and set out with both cut sides up.

3. Measure and mix together the olive oil and balsamic vinegar with the salt and pepper in the small bowl using a fork or whisk.

4. Spoon the oil and vinegar mixture onto both cut sides of the bread. Because the vinegar is dark, you can see if it is evenly distributed.

5. Spread the goat cheese onto the bottom half of the bread.

6. Layer the tomatoes, then the cucumbers, and finally the basil on top of the goat cheese. Add slices of onion if you want.

7. Put the top bread on the sandwich and press down lightly.

Either wrap the sandwich tightly in plastic wrap and refrigerate it or cut the sandwich into as many slices as you want. The slices can be held together with toothpicks. 🍅

4. Unlike cow cheeses, goat cheeses are usually not left to age, which is why they look so fresh and creamy.

5. Other ways to eat goat cheese: in a salad, on toasted bagels, in lasagna, in place of sour cream on baked potatoes, in cheesecake.

6. Besides cows and goats, other milk-producing animals used in cheese-making are sheep, buffalo, and zebu.

THE FOX AND THE GRAPES

On a hot summer's day, the sun broiling the countryside, a fox strolled through an orchard. He had nothing in mind, just ambling along.

All at once he came to a bunch of grapes that were ripening on a trellised vine.

He sniffed, suddenly both hungry and thirsty. "Just the thing for a hot summer's day."

Drawing back a few paces, the fox then ran forward and leaped into the air, snapping at the grapes with his teeth. But he missed by no more than an inch and his teeth clicked together: snip-snip-snap!

Turning around, he went a little further back, then ran forward faster, jumped higher, but–alas–missed again.

A third, a fourth, and a fifth time he tried to get that tempting morsel, but each jump was less successful than the last.

Finally, panting and perspiring under the hot sun, he walked away with his nose in the air. "I didn't want those grapes anyway," he told himself. "I'm quite sure they're sour." ⭐

Fruit Salad

Use only sweet fruit—never sour. (Serves a family or a party)

EQUIPMENT:

- sharp knife
- melon-baller (optional)
- cutting board
- rubber spatula

INGREDIENTS:

- Fruit—any kind!

Good options include: watermelon, cantaloupe, honeydew melon, pineapple, strawberries, star fruit, apples, oranges, tangerines, peaches—and of course grapes.

For the top (fruit you don't want to mix in because they are more delicate—and pretty), try one or several of these: blueberries, blackberries, raspberries, or kiwi.

DIRECTIONS:

1. Wash and prepare the fruit:

Melon: cut in half, discard the seeds, and scoop out the flesh with a melon-baller or a spoon. Melons can also be cut into cubes with a knife.

Citrus, such as oranges: peel and remove pith (white part). Section, remove seeds and cut into chunks.

Other fruits: Peel, if necessary, and cut into chunks.

2. Squeeze an orange and pour the juice over the fruit salad.

3. Mix with the rubber spatula.

4. Put topping fruit(s) on top, cover, and refrigerate until ready to eat.

VARIATIONS:

All fruit salads are different depending on the seasonal fruit available. Some fruit can be pre-cut (and even canned), but always use as much fresh fruit as possible. Putting your fruit salad in a carved out watermelon is always a welcome party treat. 🍎

4. Many insects can damage grapes: grape leafroller, climbing cutworm, flea beetles, grape berry moth, aphids, and Japanese beetles among others.
5. In the United States, 97 percent of table grapes are grown in California.
6. Grapes can be used in many ways: eaten plain; dried for raisins; made into juice, wine, jelly, and jams; or as sweeteners in other cooked products.

THE STOLEN BREAD SMELLS

O nce in a small town in the middle of the country there was a baker known far and wide as Mr. Stingy because he never gave away free samples. But as he was the finest baker around, the local people still bought bread at his shop.

Now, day after day when Mr. Stingy made his bread, the smell floated from the ovens, through the keyhole of the closed front door, and out into the street. It was that smell—delicious and enticing—that always brought buyers into his shop.

Mr. Stingy liked the fact that the smell brought people in. But one day he noticed that there was one man, with a raggedy coat and no hat, who stood outside and simply sniffed and sniffed the bread smell but did not come in to buy.

"Look at him," Mr. Stingy whispered. "Stealing my bread smells! Filling himself up—and nothing in it for me." He waved his fist at the beggar, but the man did not move.

"Get away! Get away!" shouted Mr. Stingy at the beggar. But still the man did not move. He just sniffed and sniffed some more.

At last the stingy baker could stand it no longer. He called 911 and when the police arrived, he had them arrest the beggar.

"He's a thief!" Mr. Stingy cried.

The beggar was hauled off to jail and that afternoon (this is a fairy tale after all) he was brought before a judge. The charge: theft of bread smell.

Quickly the judge made his decision. (Definitely a fairy tale!) He said to the beggar, "Have you any coins?"

The beggar reached into his worn pants pocket and pulled out a worn copper penny and one thin dime. "That's it, m'Lord."

He handed the two coins to the judge.

The judge rattled the coins and they clinked together. He turned to the baker. "Hear that?"

Confused, the baker nodded.

"That's your payment. The sound of coins as payment for the theft of smells." ⭐

Sweet-Smelling Cinnamon Bread

Smells so good your family might just sneak a whiff. (Makes 1 or 2 loaves)

EQUIPMENT:

- measuring cup
- food processor with steel blade
- measuring spoons
- pan
- rolling pin
- large bowl
- wet cloth
- loaf pan(s)

INGREDIENTS:

- 3 cups all-purpose flour (400 g)
- 1 tsp. salt
- 1¼ cups lukewarm water (290 ml)
- 1 tbsp. butter
- 1 tbsp. sugar
- 1 packet active dry yeast
- 1 tbsp. vegetable oil
- extra flour
- 2 tbsp. sugar
- 1 tsp. cinnamon

Facts about bread:
1. As far as we can determine, humans first ate a crude flat bread about 10,000 BCE. This bread was made by crushing grain into flour with a grinding stone, then adding water. This paste was cooked upon hot stones covered with hot ashes.
2. The Egyptians were the first to bake raised bread in closed ovens. Remains of loaves have been found in ancient Egyptian tombs.
3. The first bakers' guilds were in Rome in 150 BCE. Rich Romans preferred white bread to brown because it was harder to make.

DIRECTIONS:

1. Measure the flour and salt and pour into the food processor. (You can do without the processor—it'll just take more time and muscle.)

2. Melt the butter at low heat and add the water, sugar and yeast. Let sit for 5 minutes.

3. Close the food processor and turn on. Pour the water mixture through the feeding tube (the hole in the top). Let the food processor continue running until the dough is completely mixed.

4. Sprinkle some flour onto a clean work surface and on your hands and remove the dough from the food processor (carefully because the blade is sharp).

5. Knead the dough for 2 minutes, adding more flour to your hands if it is too sticky. Make the dough into a ball.

6. Coat the large bowl with the vegetable oil and place the ball of dough into it, turning once to coat with oil. Cover with a wet (but not dripping) cloth and put the bowl in a warm place so the dough can rise for one hour.

7. Preheat oven to 350 degrees.

8. Decide whether you want to make one large loaf or two smaller loaves. If you choose two, separate the dough into two pieces now.

9. Knead the dough and roll it out with the rolling pin until flat.

10. Mix the cinnamon and sugar together in a small bowl and sprinkle the mixture onto the dough.

11. Roll the dough up from each side toward the middle, tucking the unrolled ends in before you are done. Pinch the top to hold the dough together.

12. Butter the loaf pan(s) and put in the rolled dough.

13. Cook for 40 minutes for two small loaves or 50 minutes for one large loaf.

14. Serve with butter.

VARIATIONS:

You can cook this bread without adding the cinnamon sugar, just as plain bread. Or try rolling it into balls or twisting it into sticks and coating it with the cinnamon sugar.

For more great fiction and nonfiction, go to windmillbooks.com.